Uncle Bobby's Wedding

SARAH S. BRANNEN

G. P. PUTNAM'S SONS

G. P. PUTNAM'S SONS
A division of Penguin Young Readers Group.
Published by The Penguin Group.
Penguin Group (USA) Inc., 375 Hudson Street, New York, NY 10014, U.S.A.
Penguin Group (Canada), 90 Eglinton Avenue East, Suite 700, Toronto, Ontario M4P 2Y3, Canada
(a division of Pearson Penguin Canada Inc.).
Penguin Books Ltd, 80 Strand, London WC2R 0RL, England.
Penguin Ireland, 25 St. Stephen's Green, Dublin 2, Ireland (a division of Penguin Books Ltd.).
Penguin Group (Australia), 250 Camberwell Road, Camberwell, Victoria 3124, Australia
(a division of Pearson Australia Group Pty Ltd).
Penguin Books India Pvt Ltd, 11 Community Centre, Panchsheel Park, New Delhi - 110 017, India.
Penguin Group (NZ), 67 Apollo Drive, Rosedale, North Shore 0745, Auckland, New Zealand
(a division of Pearson New Zealand Ltd.)
Penguin Books (South Africa) (Pty) Ltd, 24 Sturdee Avenue, Rosebank, Johannesburg 2196, South Africa.
Penguin Books Ltd, Registered Offices: 80 Strand, London WC2R 0RL, England.

Manufactured in China by South China Printing Co. Ltd. Design by Katrina Damkoehler. Text set in Esprit.

The artist used watercolor and graphite on cold press watercolor paper to create the illustrations for this book.

Library of Congress Cataloging-in-Publication Data
Brannen, Sarah.   Uncle Bobby's wedding / Sarah S. Brannen.   p. cm.
Summary: Chloe is jealous and sad when her favorite uncle announces that he will be getting married,
but as she gets to know Jamie better and becomes involved in planning the wedding,
she discovers that she will always be special to Uncle Bobby—and to Uncle Jamie, too.
[1. Uncles—Fiction. 2. Weddings—Fiction. 3. Same-sex marriage—Fiction. 4. Homosexuality—Fiction.] I. Title.
PZ7.B737514Unc 2008   [E]—dc22   2007016550

ISBN 978-0-399-24712-5
3 5 7 9 10 8 6 4 2

The author thanks the Society of Children's Book
Writers and Illustrators for their support.

To my family,
and to all people
who love each other

Bobby was Chloe's favorite uncle.
They went for long walks together.

He took her rowing on the river.
He taught her the names of the stars.

Once they even climbed to the top of a lighthouse.

"Let's live here!" said Chloe.

"I'd like that," said Uncle Bobby.

One day, Mama had a picnic for the whole family. There were pickles and olives and cucumber sandwiches and pumpkin cookies. Bobby and his friend Jamie brought bottles of fizzy cider.

"We're getting married," said Uncle Bobby.
Mama whooped and hugged him. Daddy shook
hands with Jamie. Everyone was smiling and talking
and crying and laughing.

Everyone except Chloe.

"Mama," said Chloe, "I don't understand! How can Uncle Bobby get married?"

"Bobby and Jamie love each other," said Mama. "When grown-up people love each other that much, they want to be married."

"But," said Chloe, "Bobby is my special uncle. I don't want him to get married."

"I think you should talk to him," said Mama.

"Let's go for a walk," said Uncle Bobby. He and Chloe took their favorite path through the field.

"Why do you have to get married?" asked Chloe.

"Jamie and I want to live together and have our own family now," said Bobby.

"You want your own kids?"

"Only if they're just like you," said Bobby.

"That's a pretty good reason," said Chloe. "But—"

"But what?" said Bobby.

"I still don't think you should get married. You have ME! We can keep having fun together, like always."

"I promise we'll keep having fun together," said Bobby. "You'll always be my Chloe."

Bobby and Jamie asked Chloe to go to the ballet with them. Afterward they had ice cream sodas. Jamie imitated the ballet dancers and Chloe laughed so hard, she got soda up her nose.

Bobby and Jamie taught Chloe to sail. She fell in the water at the dock and Jamie fished her out.

After they dried her off, Chloe said,
"That was the most fun I ever had."

At night, Chloe played board games with Bobby and Jamie. They toasted marshmallows in the fireplace.

"I wish both of you were my uncles," said Chloe.

"You get your wish, sweetheart," said Bobby. "When we get married, you'll have an Uncle Jamie too."

"You'll still be my one and only Uncle Bobby, though," promised Chloe.

"And when we get married," said Jamie, "would you do us the honor of being our flower girl?"

"What kind of cake are you having?" asked Chloe.

"What kind of cake would you like?" asked Jamie.

"Carrot cake!" said Chloe.

"Carrot cake it is," said Jamie.

"Okay," said Chloe. "I'll be your flower girl."

On the day of the wedding, Chloe put on her new dress. Everyone was excited and busy. Uncle Bobby lost the rings. Jamie couldn't tie his bow tie.

Chloe found the rings in Bobby's jacket pocket. She helped Jamie with his tie. And she helped Mama put the perfect finishing touches on the wedding cake.

"We're ready!" said Chloe.

An afternoon breeze cooled the garden. Daisies
and buttercups bloomed in the grass and the air
smelled like roses. Cousins, grandparents and friends
watched Chloe walk down the path holding her
bouquet. Mama sang a wedding song.

Bobby and Jamie got married.

"That was the best wedding ever," said Chloe.
"I planned it all from the beginning."
The band started to play. She jumped up and
grabbed Uncle Bobby's and Uncle Jamie's hands.

Everyone danced until the moon rose.